The Hare Who Lost Her Hair

This book is dedicated to my beautiful daughter. Before you knew much more than the alphabet, you became aware of a harsh reality. You have been my biggest inspiration to get well and my inspiration for this book. To my husband who stayed strong, gave middle-of-the-night hugs to pull me out of despair and gives me the amazing gift of unconditional love. Thank you to my mother and father for taking over responsibilities so that I could rest and receive treatment. And, additional gratitude goes to my mother for reading all my drafts, witnessing the evolution of this book and for encouraging me to leap over the moon and publish it.

The Hare Who Lost Her Hair
Copyright 2013 by Amy V. Leonard

ISBN: 1489590056
ISBN-13: 978-1489590053

LCCN: 2013910227

CreateSpace Independent Publishing Platform
North Charleston, SC, USA

Dandelion seeds fluttered like snowflakes across an open field. A family of hares hopped through the wishing seeds, making their wildest wishes.

"I wish for carrots as big as trees," said one hare.
"I wish for cheetah speed," said another.
A brown hare named Hope said, "I wish I could hop over the moon. And I wish for golden fur."
"That's too many wishes!" her sister argued.

"Okay, then I'll pick the moon!" replied Hope.

The moon must have heard her wish. It came to visit a short
time later. Hope had never seen the moon so big. So round.
She wondered why it had fallen from the sky.
"This is your chance!" her sister cried.

But, sadly, Hope did not feel like
jumping the moon that night.
She was too tired.

Instead, she nestled in some grass
and fell fast asleep.

When she awoke the next morning
the moon had gone back to the sky, far away.

Soon Fall arrived and the field turned gold and red with
fluffy piles of leaves. The other hares excitedly hopped
over the leaves like popcorn popping in a hot pan.
This was the hares' favorite time of year.
But Hope felt too tired to join them.

She was sick.
She hadn't felt well for a long time.

Her family was worried. This was more than a flu or a cold. Hope was really sick, and she needed special medicine. Her family told her to visit the Mysterious Stream in the Forest of Mirrors. Drinking water from the stream could heal a very sick animal. But most hares never went there. They heard it was a confusing place where you might not find your way back home.

Hope wanted to feel well again.
She wanted to play. So she gathered
all her courage and left the next morning.

She traveled for several days, struggling over rocky ledges and through dark, root-twisted tunnels.

She was weak and weary. She often thought of turning back and going home.

Finally she reached the Forest of Mirrors. The trees towered above her like giants. They made her feel small and fragile. Their leaves cast reflections like mirrors.

With every turn, her reflection stared back at her. She was frightened, lost and tired. "I want to go home!" she cried.

Suddenly a large, white owl swooped down from the trees and pointed the way. Hope followed him through poisonous mushroom patches and over jagged rocks to a murky stream.

The Mysterious Stream! Hope drank the water, but
it tasted awful. She held her breath and drank it anyway.
She knew it was her only chance to get better.

The wise owl never left her side. He quietly led her through the forest and back home.

At first the odd water didn't seem to work.
All she could do was sleep.
She felt terribly sick.

Then Hope began to lose her fur.
She lost little by little each day until...

she had lost all of it!
Without her fur,
she felt shy.
She wanted to hide
under the bushes.

"I wished for golden fur, not NO fur!"
she scolded the dandelions.

Hope's sister made a sweater of colorful field grass.
The sweater made Hope feel prettier and happier.
Hope came out of her hiding places, but she did not
want to go back to the forest and drink the water that
made her lose her fur.

Her family said, "The Mysterious Stream does more than take away your fur. It also heals."
Hope thought about that. Her losing fur was a sign the sickness in her body might be getting smaller, too.
"Besides, your fur can grow back!" the little hare encouraged.

Hope looked at herself
in a nearby pond.
The image was still her even if she looked different.
She was still the same hare inside.
She still wanted to hop over the moon.

Hope knew she had to keep drinking the strange water.
It was her best chance for getting well, which is what she
wished for the most. So she followed the owl to the stream,
week after week
after week.

It seemed like the Mysterious Stream would never help. But, in time, Hope started to feel better. Day by day she began to grow a little fur and hop a little higher.

Soon she had a fluffy coat of fur again. She was well!

Hope thought things couldn't get any better. But, then the
moon returned. Hope knew not to waste another moment.
Feeling stronger and braver than ever before,
she raced to the edge of the field and made
her most ambitious leap.

As she splashed through the moon's light,
her fur turned a stunning golden color.
The hares gasped at her beauty.

The glow lasted just for a moment. But the color of her fur no longer mattered. Whether she had brown, gold or no fur at all, Hope was happy just the same.

She jumped and exclaimed, "Being well again is the best wish to ever come true!" Her family cheered.

From that day onward her sister believed in the possibility of many wishes coming true. And, in the power of Hope.

Author's Note

Juggling life as a stay-at-home mom, freelance writer and real estate agent, I was diagnosed with stage 3 breast cancer in April 2010. I was 38 years old and my daughter was three years old.

My treatment plan included a bilateral mastectomy, breast reconstruction, eight rounds of chemotherapy, radiation and hormonal treatment.

One of my biggest concerns about treatment was how to explain my impending physical changes to my daughter, especially the loss of my long hair. I searched for books to help me explain this situation, but I found the library and book stores lacking appropriate literature for a very young audience. In addition to honest discussions, I made up funny stories for my daughter about animals or people losing their hair. She loved the light-hearted stories and they seemed to put her at ease with my changes.

I hope this simple tale inspires your own family and provides some comfort to your little ones about the physical changes from chemo. May God bless you and your family and provide the healing you need.

To contact the author for scheduling interviews, signings, readings or special events, email booksabouthope@gmail.com